MISDEMEANOR CITY

SUMEET KUMAR

Sumeet Kumar

Sumeet Kumar , A adult who experiences many phases of life , a well known writer and a writer of new era . In reality he is a writter as well as singer (as a hobby) and a standup comedian . Very exciting and interesting fact about him is that he is author of New era i.e. he starts his journey of writing at the age when he was going to schools to get the study . His streak of 100 books will be the great achievement for him in future. His some famous works i.e. Maturity Of Love (Genre - Love),Privacy For Dream (Genre

- Middle Class), Army Squad ofLove (Genre- The Seperation of Army Love), 5 Days of Love(Genre- Temporarily Love), The Endearment Of Love(Genre - Historical Era Of Love), Social Destruction Indo-Pak (Genre - The Story of The Love At The Time Of Division Of India And Pakistan), Middle Class Soul (Genre - The Dreams of Middle Class), The Accursed Kanatpur (Genre -The Horrific Story Of A Village), Wrong Number (Genre -The Suspenseful Physco Killer Story), The Secrecy OfDeadly Midnight (Genre - The Suspense About a Crime),Fragile Religious Of Death (Genre- The Death Of A TrustfulPerson), Nature Vs Science (Genre - The Future Battle Between Nature And Science In A Horrific Way), Generic Man (Genre - The Dream of I.I.T), The Unconsious 12 Hours(Genre - The Illusion At Stage Of Comma), The StrangeBurden (Genre - The Burden Of Love) , Her Existence (Genre- The Female Pain In The Society) , Jockstrap Prize (Genre -The True Story Of A National Athlete) , H Man [Hindi] (Genre - Superhero Tragic Story), H Man [English] (Genre - Superhero Tragic Story) , Maturity Of Love [English] (Genre - Love) and many more are available on various geners on the offcial platform of **Amazon, Flipkart and Notionpress.** You can buy them from there.

Contents

Acknowledgements   *vii*

1. Silent Peace   1

2. The Crime Of Dark   8

3. The Suspectivity   20

Acknowledgements

Sumeet Kumar

Special Thanks to **Aman Kumar** who worked so hard in the preparation of this book. He has continually put with my passive voice, omission of words, and late night calls. You have been wonderful. Thanks to him for his precious time in reviewing proposals , individual chapters and early drafts, along with his suggestions on the applicability of the material to the world.

I

Silent Peace

Crime is such a sweetheart that does not leave our pursuit till the dying dam, say it is in the past, it says in the future, its punishment in the past remains the same in the past and even in the future and the past, the characters of the feet who commit crimes change their lives.

Goes and the gift of dreams is not the fault, they leave it long ago when the time changes, people often change and their relationship is like a happy dream, which is only for some time. Try to be with you, feet will leave your feet at the right time There is some baryon of the question which is still groping my me every time that after all where does the crime begin From a farg, it means to someone, it is understood that from those lamps, in whose shadow he has erased all the innocence of his childhood, which He still tries to remember that there are some crimes that have not been prescribed in the world, yet we consider it as a crime and there are some crimes which are clearly visible, so the feet are often their fault. Do not consider it a crime, in the eyes of the world, if you have lost your humanity, then you have become a human and if you have become a human being, then there is a difference between the two. the destruction and cruelty worshiped by Ravana, who was a demon, and some people still worship him, so some people make effigies of him and burn them on the day of Ramnauvi. There is also a demon and the person who is not wise is also a demon, the good has only the same price as humanity and the evil has the same price as we can not know, science is also cruel and natural because if we have In return, we will get the same hatred as we have done for them. It is clear that there is a reason for every crime, and behind every crime, his need, who has the power, he is also wicked and the one who is wise is also savage, the difference is such that the cruelty of the wise is never clearly visible. The cruelty of the person who has the power is clearly visible, they say that even after death, if something remains in someone's mind, then it becomes a curse when a fearful says goodbye to his anger, then many logs are present at that time.

He lives in the fire of graveyard, he also thinks about Surrey, in whose flame all his bad and bad deeds get burnt and become bash if the charity of something remains alive after that, then the punishment of the yaadis remains. There is nothing else. Logs often say that I am alive, I don't care about us, and if we are killed, then keep the dose and happiness in the fire of graveyard, you will create a new world of your own, maybe this thing can be true because every one of it The word is right, the way the human race has made its world, the way we have our own world, every wall of it brings alive the same moments of our past. In which there is no human interest involved, only those sacrifices of sacrifice are famous, which we cannot erase from history even by saying that someone has killed for the sake of a farg, then someone told the state for some money. Somebody's woman's and her feet don't stop it, it's not even a matter that our ancestors didn't belong to humanity.

There is no one's share in a crime, nor does he initiate a male crime in someone's spirit, there is no such story that has no beginning in the beginning and if we improve its complexity in the share of crime. If you try, it is also the beginning of the same story, one who has a sweet heart, which people call by many names, compulsions, wealth, love, friendship, kindship, vanity and even outside surgery, such a donation is a gift that is present in the stake can't try to undefined some people make history so then Some history is made, we have heard such things many times, even after this, there are some logs that make history and are also found in some other history, some words are such that in the beginning, aunt's identity looks like feet.

There is such a beginning from the real world, the story of which has not been made till date. Tries to erase that which we can't even try to forget by saying, feet we try to know it all the time, there is also a curiosity, I too if the teacher has made every foundation of his ruin, then it started Where are people in the end why people are afraid of it, who is this undefined If people do not understand human evidence, then it is a big deal that person would know his habit and his nature very well and if the person do not know him, then they probably try. It is said that the beginning of any war does not happen on one side, whenever it happens, it is only two-way, the foot is its beginning and And the digestion of the intestine is very different because there are some logs which start it, then some person try to enter it, there is such a boundary between the two feet, whose words and feelings destroy a person.

Occupation of someone, when the log makes someone a king, then the citizens of that king trust that he will take away our sorrows from us and it is also necessary for the representative that he should help his people.

Humanity of human witness does not see cruelty nor the hidden meaning behind it. Only two such places in life are famous where those moments of peace are found, which a human's heart can never forget to forget, the first mother's love And there is a lot of difference between the feet of the other tomb, on one side there is the gaur of the male mother which gives us life and peace and on the one hand, the gaur of the male tomb which gives us death, the feet of the tomb can never compare with them.

Nor can the education and knowledge of any witness

compare to it, their love is the same, feet are the same in charity, one rude soul says goodbye to the other. Adopts rudeness, Well it has become a matter of a good path and life, whose intestine has no boundaries, nor is there any part of the beginning. It is the big fault of childhood memories, because it is the beginning of any crime. There is a heart that we are so far away from that we never understand it, if some curvy friends have made their home in someone's mind since childhood, then it is obviously the right thing that his friends become poison by making him cough.

She is ready to inflict pain due to which her innocence is ready to be taken away from her at a happy time and later a time also comes that the place which we give our homes and say protected is happy. moment becomes death for us, in the same way, there are many aspects of crime, by seeing which we can try to understand that where it started, we can never digest its intestine, this is because death is only a limit, not the intestine Many persons come for the same crime and many go away, only a few logs are there, those who leave their arc, say that their beginning is good for humanity. This cruelty has happened. There are some fears which get filled with time and there are also such fears that increase the feet.
Because it is a poison that we can get out of our hearts once Know that because his syrup is invisible, we can feel it, the feet can never digest him and the day he comes to know, our life does not stay with us, in the beginning of such a question in front of all of you. I am the one whose welfare is a bit strange and his wish has also been seen in time, has anyone ever tried to see him in the future, now people also know what a crazy person he is, even if

someone sees how time comes: Foot history has been lost that often those who think the world is crazy, they do something that after that the whole world scolds us. Just like we ourselves To look at means to see our own gross, we use it to repeat itself in a similar way, do not understand the meaning? They say if someone's beginning was in the past, then it is time At the same time, his anxiety is also a problem in the future and the past, now the question is, how are time and time so attached to each other that time looks at its strange eyes, we see only what we are in reality and The mirror also brings the sweet pecan in front of us, which we are in reality, in the way of time, its identity is the same, which is exactly like our face, in reality, if I say one thing, then the pecan of time never changes, it is a changing log and We only talked about his love and happiness in those three parts, whose bailout is actually only one.

"For Identity of Love what i will talk about
the winning that i have in my luck have been lost
And What type of politics i will talk about
In a incident that have been lost

Every Pain have been healed by the time
But her memories had driven my mind
The Person to whom i want to forget
Become a precious gold for my mind"

.Even if a person gets murdered, his deeds never die, he says that he is dead, he stays with him all the time and works to move him back and forth only by staying close to him, this is a kind of habit that people have to do then It seems when he forgets everything and goes out in search of his own identity because the fear of the grave is fulfilled only when someone's soul is free for disrespecting him and body is imprisoned, similarly this is the story of a hero and a villain whose life is ruined. She was like steel whom people also understood as Ravana and Ram too because time had done such an enmity with a witness in which every one of his friends has been spoiled, which he used to appreciate and also used to tell him that logs are never bad.

Nor is their love ever bad, the feet that they get educated everywhere from some harsh words of society, perhaps they get mixed in their mind like a poison, in childhood we never think about what debt we mean next. How will we carry forward the life that we have got for being born in the world of God, as soon as the thinking increases, the bailout of fear also increases and when both of them If the hatred increases, then crime and humanity also begins We all need to be trained to be a traveller.

II

The Crime of Dark

It is said that we understand the value of time when we leave our followers with us, when we try to take care of ourselves in a bad condition, they do the work of religion of karma, whose humanity is on its feet, where the patient lives.

There is only one enmity, often those whose love is clearly visible from the education of the face, they often start such a crime, even after saying that we can never erase our mind, pain and fear like: Very close to each other, just like human beings Thought and its fanna are also very close to each other because in the world the thinking of human race never stops at the same time, like the earth, it keeps roaming everywhere where it also gets good condition and bad feet also some logs like this.

There are also those who make them their profession, that means VPR, and the beginning of VPR is when there is a beginning in the mind, this person says that those who are rich are becoming richer and those who are poor.

And are getting poorer and those who speak these words are neither rich nor poor because their thinking is the first, which is clearly ahead in their life. He has got the training to grow, why will he come back because with the passage of time, he does not only see his compulsions, he has also seen his immense wealth, if he wants to move forward, why would he leave him and go to such a destination where he is not happy? Will not be able to move forward, some person would be very rich because they have wealth, bungalows, cars and if we look on the other side, then those who have got such a place in the thinking of society from which they can never leave even saying that means The society is not able to cross the line, they also know how rich they are in their gathering as compared to them, because even if they do not have immense wealth, they have that love, that is peace and the biggest thing is the wealth By which everything in the world can be bought.

Now-a-days people also say that we can buy someone's love with money. This is what is to be bought from the market because this is not something that is sold in any shop, 100 or 150. Why am I saying undefined what is the meaning of all undefined and why is it related to the story of the child witness and why am I including it in such a bailout.

"If I have faith on religion , so I will not know the
meaning of human
There will be a relationship of brother and sister
but i will not know them
My life is exactly in depressed as of human
There will be a need of dream but i will not won
them"

Well, the testimony about which I am going to tell you all, his wish is also true and no one is aware of the story as well because every single word of it was caused by someone's death.MEERUT (UTTAR PRADESH) 19 JUNE 2004.

I am writing in the handwriting of the teacher in the pages, why the unfinished story in which I am going to tell everyone, the germ in which I am going to write it was done in this way, many people will be aware of Meerut city and many people They go to roam and live in the same way, let me tell you that there is a population of about 17 lakhs in this city, it is probably more than that, but one thing is simple in all that they can leave their city Meerut to their feet. The heart can never go away because if it was only about a city, then maybe he could have left the people of death, to say that he can make its friends even worse than himself, foot talk is not just about the city Yes, the sparks that we have built and the spark started by our ancestors has also become a fire against the British in 1857, and what about Meerut, Meerut is the place where Mother Yamuna's yadis and Kali The strong feelings of the river are associated with its effect, the water that we accept, it is the same charity and that the sweets that fill your life with sweetness, it is I'm not talking about anyone else, I'm only talking about revri gajak, whoever I see enough, go on saying, by the way, if you start telling about your love, then the whole number will also be enough, in my education autobiography, some new bottles, new bottles Not connected like: everyone's life is common and dreams are common Nor do I want to be a big person because someone's Sikh still remembers in the mind of my father, because all the tiles I have got since childhood have been given to him, his principles, his word, his ideal and his I am also proud, I do not say it at all in bottles, this is what our mother says, by the way my father is not that rich, put such a flight in every one of my dreams, which in no time can stop the light of reality.

What I definitely need is one thing that I want to say about them which I have never said to them and maybe until they write this. Until then, I will go very far from my life, and maybe my anger will also be separated from my fear, I am not afraid of feeling in my feet, because father used to tell us every time such things, that whenever you are in some way, you It is time to understand that whatever you have done, say that it is absolutely right for you, it is absolutely right for someone else, maybe their words were right because even though what I have done in the eyes of the society, it is probably wrong to a large extent. And rightly so, because this is such a destination, whose beginning connects me with those two paths, which I am very unaware of, before I become the story of death, I tell my unfinished things, which I have never been to anyone except I myself have decided the way of my ruin long ago, still it is necessary to write the bail and way again of the thing which I had started in a long time, so the day I saw my ruin with my eyes, it is 19th June It is 2004, everyone in the house was very happy, on this day mother had brought Aarti's group and father was all saying that my Akshu should be given nine.

Have got curry, the day he had spread lies in the whole locality, he was so happy that seeing his happiness, my tears were coming out that means how can someone love someone till the limit, at the time papa was holding my hands to everyone. I was trying to say that my dreams were finally fulfilled. If you are successful in life, then all those people say that my hard work and my passion are the real passion for my success, they say that behind every man there is a woman's hand, on the right day on the feet, for the first time. I used to say to prove my shoes because behind me are the hands of both of them who gave me love and a good education too, in a middle class family, when anyone gets a job, then it is not work for the members of left during any festival.

It would have been, and that was not useful for my family during any festival, the feet say that there is a specialty of every festival that their happiness too It is like a guest who will stay in your gathering and your house for a few moments, after that like a traveler, she leaves your house and goes to some other house, that too in a house where the walls are also connected to those deserted then.

There is a place where we can't keep our steps even after saying it, on this day I had seen the whole world in a single moment, that too in my father's eyes at the time, I was not aware of some flicker, which I was going to get in part, whose bailout Neither demanded nor ever said, because our luck makes us compete with those paths, whose destination was never present in our part, nor do we say to walk on their paths, yet they have their beginning and those paths There are also feet, no one knows about this My son will do, the shelters on which I have built the foundation, now he will make my axis and now I am not worried about anything because now my To handle the compulsions and the circumstances of my house, I have my son, my son, I have not told my family, nor my family's well-being, if it has already started, then I will give everyone the blessings of the father.

Rajesh Pathak who is the head principal of our house, which means my father and my whole world, Lata Pathak, who is my mother and the foundation of our relationship and home, also Samar Pathak, who is the naughtiest person of my house whom we all love very much means my Mother's beloved beta and my father's life and my happiness deserved too bash enough ,my small right world Papa is a ticket collector by profession, that too in railways and my mother is a housewife and the satan of our house whom I teach in work and bat Likes the tune of the ball and the melody of the ball, means that he plays cricket a lot, that means since childhood, he has decided that he will become a big cricketer one day, my dreams were not big, my hopes were big, dad used to say every time. They were that even if your job is small, even if it is a profession, whatever work you do, you should do it for respect.

Because no one will get big earning from this in your own

share, nor does anyone get great success in life, dad principles is still in my heart, I know that now she is not adore, yet there is a saying that My world may be the same for a day as before Well, the beginning of it was a human witness whose world was very different from me and my world was very different from that, I want to reveal the name of the same witness who had given the sheet of my happiness in a moment, the story of a human grave, which I say I could not even adopt it, when my father was doing my batis in the whole locality, then such a witness saw feet in our house, looking beyond our happiness in those gatherings, the doors of each and every room started closing.

I knew him and neither mother had ever seen him, his father's happiness had turned into sorrow in an instant, there was such silence in the whole locality. The shadow had passed for a long time, which I could not understand even after saying it, and why was my father so angry with her and why was she so silent, who was that witness and why my father was standing in front of her bowing her head because I was the first I had seen such a condition in my whole life because before this dad had never bowed his head in front of anyone even for us and who is this Chaudry Dharamjit Singh and who is the true enmity hidden behind his name. dad then asked many times that dad who is this undefined even at some time he was telling me nothing beta you go inside the house I still tried to ask, he didn't say anything even at that time he bash kept talking so much that enough Now go inside, I come in a while, I might have gone disrespectful at the time, my condition would not have been like this, if the feet had gone, then the condition of my family before would not have been possible days, mother was already inside feet Summer was out, that time was only back from the practice session that when he saw his knee and foot and saw that gun, he also saw his legs and feet.

The man could not control himself at the time and because of his words, he murdered Chaudarya Dharamjit Singh, his feet and legs, before we tried to save him, before this, the father tried to stop him, he had shown that immense love for him. then the whole community and his principles were not different, feet say that there is some thing which is different from blood, when Dharamjit Singh died, father was very scared, he was beating enough Samar at that time and he was speaking Were and were telling all of us that soon take your sari essential things because we are going to leave that city neither we knew this thing at the time nor did the mother know what is going on. Yes, we were not unaware that we have died in some trouble, that means the death of Dharamjit Singh, because his death was due to my younger brother who was still a minor at the time, and it was not even in the present time.

What happened was that Samar had murdered him because we were all disrespectful to the feet, dad and Samar on that time it gonna were out of time, which meant that such a condition had come, that too for a while. When I went inside, on one side the police door and on the other side the beginning of such a war which was one sided, now we were not unaware of which gathering was going to start, dad enough told us all to get out of bad condition, that's why he just Our clothes and our bare feet are not tied to our own feet and I have been told that if possible, come back to the mat sometime and take care of your mother and your younger brother, say I am stay maybe, you are talking again and again and you worry. I will see all this

and nothing will happen to Samar
Means my words are not as much as they seem, and
neither is my condition because I myself was trying to
understand what happened after all.
I knew that my brother had killed him by mistake and
at that time a sub inspector was, then he could have
handled this situation, at that time I would have asked
some questions that why his killing him like this..

And maybe I would have been given a suspension order for
a few days, why didn't my father understand these bottles
and why should we be afraid and I Why should the family
leave their shears, our condition would have improved in
the short term, my family would have broken because if
Samar was in jail, I could not wear the uniform even after
saying that because I do not get that respect, I have used
these words. For a long time, I hid everyone that I am the
same, in a short time the police had also come to take me
to take Samar with his seventeen, because that was the
first day of my duty, when he killed Dharamjit dead body:
See, even people were scared at the time, that means their
voice was not coming out and they were asking me who
killed him sir undefined Now no one can save maybe the
meerut city is not safe from his father's fear and killed
him.

Who is undefined, many questions have been asked to him
at the time, who is this, do you know this sir, who does not
know the goon, whoever killed him, his father will not
leave him, that's how long the father had come and we He
was telling everyone to get healthy and was explaining to
me that you should leave your job right now and go to your
uncle's house and see Samar and others.

Take Whee to your mother, she will come in few days, by then everyone came to know in this news in the whole locality that Samar had killed Dharamjeet not by anyone else. Mujseh said this thing that sir your father is saying right now everyone should go away this time and maybe try to come back sometime because this was the only beta of Chaudary Anoop Singh and instead of his blood, he was the whole locality. Will change it into a keep that happiness will turn into such a silence that even by saying that you will not be able to bring him again to the festival Didn't come means the whole locality had come to the feet, that's why I didn't think much at the time and I did what my father told me at that time, I knew his condition in the feet, I had read my eyes at that time that these words which he had told once We did it to us, it is never going to be complete, it means that the father will never return because at that time the people of left had given me this thing clearly. That Choudhary Anoop Singh is not going to leave anyone, leave as soon as you can, and Papa was not just asking me to go away, he had felt his grief at the time, which told him to go to the grave. I was about to make famous in the gathering, that's why I didn't ask anything to him at that time. I was not going to leave my heart, that's why I told my father that we will all go away, before that, father, you sit with me for a while and drink water first, I put chloroform tablets in it after sacrificed my life.

Whose father fainted in a short time after drinking because some things I know about my father better than him, he had sacrificed his life to save us when he asked us to go and saying no to himself He also decided for his family that even if I get death, there is a scratch in my family's foot in the part. Won't let me come, feet say that even if you listen to the door of happiness, the dark changes never hide your feet, when I had two paths, I should sacrifice myself for this man, the father in which I see my whole world. , I knew very well that Chaudarya Anoop Singh would take revenge, this river of blood would not stop because the statue which was told to me by everyone, the love that I had given birth to at a very young time, probably this thing is in my mind every time. Was wandering that I have to keep my family away from my shadow by any means, I had thought that if duty had already died, then I would die after finishing this whole story because I will never forget my family. Even if my death is not written in the part, because only me and my family knew this thing at the time and left had some person foot Chaudry Anoop Singh did not know at all that his son was murdered by someone else. No, my younger brother has done it, that's why I started such an enmity right now that neither can my family go ahead in any way That trouble did not come, nor should my brother face any trouble, so I said only one thing at the time that I have killed Dharamjit, and he told all the person that if anyone dared to speak the truth.

I will kill him before I say so that I am dead, after all I went to the station first and then he got three ticks cut of then Bangalore and then caught mom, dad and Samar in the morning and in a short time. Went with him too because I had promised my mother that I would go with you and stay with you, we all caught the train together and never went to Bangalore with my family on foot, I knew that if I said these things directly, so they will allow me to stay in Meerut sometime, and if my father comes to his senses, he himself will remain in Meerut.

Will give it, by the way, I had bought tickets to Bangalore because she could never get close to my family even after being the shadow of chaudhary Anoop Singh.
There is also a mystery behind this in which many questions are hidden, that too undefined like a passer by.

"*You are the dark to the world of light*
The person who couldn't be described in a paper is
you
I know my time is not so good today
But the person who is the owner of this body is
you
"

III

The Suspectivity

If the journey ends, then we leave our destination too and those paths become difficult even after walking on which we have seen such condition in our life, walking on which was a gift, stopping the foot was not a blessing at all, hate is not a wall. The people says, hatred is the reason for such an enmity, due to which people forget their humanity, if they ask for revenge, then stop calling yourself human, if there is a custom of forgiveness, then kiss the steps of humanity of people It is also said that if your feet had passed, then you probably would never speak these words, would you be able to bear any pain, would we also have the same hatred that this society does, in the same way, this society is undefined, who does not know them and neither I only ever ask to be familiar with them, because the principle that they have created, I do not think that their ideals can save anyone's life, they can move someone forward, why am I doing the gifts of society, that too when I am proud.

A floor has come to the feet where my grave is ready to embrace me, there is a mystery behind it too, the love that is incomplete before the feet.

In my autobiography, first to decide his destination, we need to move forward on Singh's journey, neither day I sent my entire family to Bangalore, that too thinking that they will remain safe because neither their time No one knew nor knew to tell this to anyone, it was public in the feet that if our condition does not improve in time, then we will never be able to improve, at that time Chaudary Anoop Singh did not know at all that his son would die. It is not done and no one had given it, so I thought that before anyone would even know that Dharamjeet was killed by my brother Samar, before that
I burnt his entire fear, that too by going to a place where Foot birds also used to come very thoughtfully, that means, in a small factory which was about 15 km away from Meerut city then it was probably an oil factory which was closed for a long time, and before that Anop Singh knew this. Moving that his only son had died, before that I went

to meet him for some time. It was also realized that his son's death was due to my brother, so he tried to kill my family, as soon as he went to his house to share that Dharamjeet had died, even before that his father were present and both of them were doing each other's baths, that too in such a tone that I was completely surprised to see, even before what I was going to say in the bottles, dad said that surgery baton, Chaudary Anoop Singh then, The feet which he had said at the time, perhaps there was such an enmity that he could never hear those candles from his ears, I wish he did not know his love, whose face was taught to me as a love for me, and he even said that in return. After all, what was said by the father to Chaudary Anoop Singh? In this case, while trying to proceed with his revenge, the people of Chaudary Anup Singh saw me and he also fired half of his tune because Chaudary Anoop Singh I thought that I had killed his son, it is not such a thing that I could not fight him at the time, the bullets he fired at me at that time Had he told me to die, he could have given him even in reply, he could have taken revenge on him as well, as he was in peace at the time. That too was a witness to him, whom I had spent my whole world with, not only God had asked him, the tone of the pain that he had handed over to me at the same time, even by saying that he freed himself from his pain and his pain. I could not have lost hope, had lost my life, even if my life was with me, I could not even say goodbye to him at that time because the father who taught me to walk by holding a finger, taught me every one of my feelings and habits in such a way. Seeing the happiness of the feet, I used to explain myself as protected, today every one of his memories is trying to make me hurt himself.

"

I have heard that the condition of people changes with time. "

The world has changed, after all, why did he do such an undefined thing, what was the reason for him in my love for him that he saved one of his sons in another way He was murdered alive, and I am probably not even his own blood. I had made a thousand promises to go around the whole world by sitting on my shoulders and feet, today my father took my world to China, well, these things were probably not in a condition to say at the time, I have been able to ride my feet now that I have made myself capable of their Even pain now gives me a story to live with all the time.20 minutes before ....When I went to meet Chaudarya Anoop Singh then that too to tell him that someone was guilty of killing your son, then at that time I ducked the father ,

at first I was surprised to see him because I had spent my time. I had given him foil, in which drugs were also found and he drank it in front of me and he had also fainted at the time, how did he get so fast: Jagga I had thought at the time that the news of Dharamjeet's death Chaudya Anoop Singh has felt his feet, before this he tried to think of something else, he used to tell his family to be safe, I saw something that seeing that my eyes were also imprisoned in the darkness at the same time. I was hugging and at that time my father told Chaudary Anoop Singh that I have killed his son (means Akshya Pathak undefined ? And he is deliberately trapping my summer in his water that you feel like Chaudarya) We have killed your son, it is not even my blood, it is the birth of some dirty drain worm, I have killed him on the way. It was ....pre - planned work which did not dare to hear anything further enough so much society: It had happened that it cheats itself, that means I had seen such a reality in myself that I was unable to say what to do. For those who have already decorated my grave in their gathering, for those who have given me all the happiness, that love, that love, that love, and everything whose charity I can't even write feet to get, It is said that a family is a hot one who stays with you in every condition, never lets you down in your every trouble and says why the grave is not ready, his feet for death even his power, even at the slightest time, you stop in the tomb till he Relationship be with you, I ran away after all, because the beginning of the battle was on one side. undefined By the way, before that I would be angry in front of those relationships whose shadows used to fill my fears, I want to say something because I want to do my best. I had written that I am not going to win from him, this is the fate of him, what I have given in his share, that too for the love of adore who has given me a lot of love, may be the last journey, before that in Mahabharata, Vasudev Krishna told Arjuna.

then Said this thing if you are in favor of religion, then take your precautions and fight with your family, say his bail, now I say to lose my part in shish jung because I can fight the whole world with my mother's love.

"

Catch my hand because i am sinking in the dark
Everywhere i go i feel a heart with a evil of the
dark"